헨젤과 그레텔

Hansel and Gretel

Retold by Manju Gregory
Illustrated by Jago

Korean translation by Yun Young-Min

MANTRA LINGUA

옛날에 가난한 나뭇꾼이 살았어요. 그에게는 두 아이가 있었어요. 오빠는 헨젤, 여동생은 그레텔이었지요. 그 때는 불행이도 굶주림이 온 세상에 퍼져 있었어요.
어느날 저녁 아버지는 새 어머니에게 한숨을 쉬며, "이제 우리가 먹을 곡식이 없구려."
"제말을 잘 들어 보세요." 새 엄마가 나쁜 꾀를 생각해 냈어요.
"아이들을 숲속에 내다 버리죠. 그 후엔 아이들이 알아서 살아갈 거예요."
"하지만 산짐승에게 잡아 먹힐수도 있지않소!" 나뭇꾼은 눈물을 흘렸어요.
"다 같이 굶어 죽을순 없잖아요?" 그녀는 말했어요.
그리곤 그녀는 마음이 약한 그를 조르고 졸라 허락을 받아냈어요.

Once upon a time, long ago, there lived a poor woodcutter with his wife and two children. The boy's name was Hansel and his sister's, Gretel. At this time a great and terrible famine had spread throughout the land. One evening the father turned to his wife and sighed, "There is scarcely enough bread to feed us."
"Listen to me," said his wife. "We will take the children into the wood and leave them there. They can take care of themselves."

"But they could be torn apart by wild beasts!" he cried.
"Do you want us all to die?" she said. And the man's wife went on and on and on, until he agreed.

두 아이들은 배가 고파 잠에 들지 못하고 있었어요.
이야기를 엿들은 그레텔은 눈물을 뚝뚝 떨어뜨렸어요.
"걱정하지마," 헨젤이 말하기를, "우리가 다시 돌아올 방법을 알아."
헨젤은 살금살금 정원으로 나갔어요. 달빛을 햇빛삼아 은동전과 같이 밝게
빛나는 하얀 조약돌을 주머니에 가득 채웠어요. 산길에 떨어뜨려 다시
돌아올 수있는 표시로 쓰려고요. 그리고는 방으로 돌아와 그레텔을
안심시켰어요.

The two children lay awake, restless and weak with hunger.
They had heard every word, and Gretel wept bitter tears.
"Don't worry," said Hansel, "I think I know how we can save ourselves."
He tiptoed out into the garden. Under the light of the moon, bright white pebbles shone like silver coins on the pathway. Hansel filled his pockets with pebbles and returned to comfort his sister.

다음 날 아침 해도 뜨기전 새 어머니는 두 아이를 깨웠어요.
"어서 일어나거라, 숲으로 나무하러 가자꾸나. 여기 빵을 하나씩 줄테니, 한 번에다
먹진 말거라."
가족은 길을 떠났고, 헨젤은 자주 뒤를 돌아봐 집으로 돌아오는 길을 눈여겨 보았어요.
"뭘 자꾸 돌아보니?" 아버지는 소리쳐 물었어요.
"그냥 지붕에 앉아있는 작은 하얀 고양이에게 손 흔들어 인사하는 거예요."
"엉뚱하기는!" 새 어머니가 말했어요. "저건, 아침 햇살에 비쳐 하얗게
보이는 굴뚝이야."
헨젤은 조심스럽게 하얀 조약돌을 하나하나 떨어뜨렸어요.

Early next morning, even before sunrise, the mother shook Hansel and Gretel awake.
"Get up, we are going into the wood. Here's a piece of bread for each of you, but don't eat it all at once."
They all set off together. Hansel stopped every now and then and looked back towards his home.
"What are you doing?" shouted his father.
"Only waving goodbye to my little white cat who sits on the roof."
"Rubbish!" replied his mother. "Speak the truth. That is the morning sun shining on the chimney pot."
Secretly Hansel was dropping white pebbles along the pathway.

깊은 숲속에 이르러 아버지와 새 어머니는 아이들을 도와
불을 지폈어요.
"불이 잘 타오르니 여기서 자고 있거라." 새 어머니가
말했어요. "그리고 우리가 데리러 올때가지 절대 다른
곳에 가면 안된다."
두 아이는 불 가까이 앉아 작은 빵을 먹었어요.
그리곤 곧 깊은 잠에 들었어요.

They reached the deep depths of the wood where the parents helped
the children to build a fire.
"Sleep here as the flames burn bright," said their mother. "And make
sure you wait until we come to fetch you."
Hansel and Gretel sat by the fire and ate their little pieces of bread.
Soon they fell asleep.

두 아이가 깨어났을땐 어두운 밤이었어요.
그레텔이 엉엉 울며, "우린 이제 집에 어떻게 돌아가?"
"둥근달이 환하게 떠 오를때까지 조금만 기다려," 헨젤이 말했어요.
"그러면 조약돌을 비출거야."
그레텔은 달이 어둠을 환이 비추기만을 기다렸어요. 그레텔은 오빠에
손을 꼭 잡고 달빛에 비친 조약돌을 찾으며 걸었어요.

When they awoke the woods were pitch black.
Gretel cried miserably, "How will we get home?"
"Just wait until the full moon rises," said Hansel. "Then we will see the shiny pebbles."
Gretel watched the darkness turn to moonlight. She held her brother's hand and together
they walked, finding their way by the light of the glittering pebbles.

두 아이는 다음날 아침이 되서야 집을 찾아 올수 있었어요.
그레텔이 집문을 열었을땐, 계모도 놀랐지만, "숲속에서
그렇게 오래자면 어떻하니? 난 너희들이 집을 못 찾을까
걱정했단다."
계모는 믿을 수 없어 화가났지만 나뭇꾼은 기뻤어요.
아버지는 아이들을 산속에 버린것을 후회했었어요.

시간은 또 흘렸어요. 또 곡식이 없어 가족이 굶주릴때였어요.
어느날 밤 계모가 속삭이는 말을 들었어요.
"이 번엔 더 깊은 숲속에 버리면 다시는 찾아오지 못할거예요."
헨젤은 다시 정원에 기어나가 조약돌을 주우려했지만 계모는 눈치챘듯
방문을 잠궈버렸어요.
"울지마," 헨젤은 그레텔을 달랬어요. "내가 다른 방법을 찾아 볼께.
걱정 말고 자."

Towards morning they reached the woodcutter's cottage.
As she opened the door their mother yelled, "Why have you slept so long in the woods?
I thought you were never coming home."
She was furious, but their father was happy. He had hated leaving them all alone.

Time passed. Still there was not enough food to feed the family.
One night Hansel and Gretel overheard their mother saying, "The children must go.
We will take them further into the woods. This time they will not find their way out."
Hansel crept from his bed to collect pebbles again but this time the door was locked.
"Don't cry," he told Gretel. "I will think of something. Go to sleep now."

다음날, 더 작은 빵과 전에 한번도 가보지못한 깊은 숲속으로 가고 있었어요.
헨젤은 빵조각을 하나씩 가는길에 떨어뜨렸어요. 아버지와 계모는 불을 지펴
아이들을 재웠어요.
"우리는 나무를 자르고 일을 마치면 너희들을 데리러 올테니 편히들 자고
있거라." 계모는 거짓말을 했어요.
그레텔의 빵을 나눠 먹은 아이들은 아버지와 계모가 돌아 올때까지 기다리고
또 기다렸지만, 아무도 오지 않았어요.
"달이 떠 빵조각들을 비추면 집에 돌아갈수 있을거야," 헨젤이 말했어요.
달은 떠 올랐지만 빵조각들을 찾을수 없었어요.
새들과 숲속 짐승들이 먹어 버렸던 거예요.

The next day, with even smaller pieces of bread for their journey, the children were led to
a place deep in the woods where they had never been before. Every now and then Hansel
stopped and threw crumbs onto the ground.
Their parents lit a fire and told them to sleep. "We are going to cut wood, and will fetch
you when the work is done," said their mother.
Gretel shared her bread with Hansel and they both waited and waited. But no one came.
"When the moon rises we'll see the crumbs of bread and find our way home," said Hansel.
The moon rose but the crumbs were gone.
The birds and animals of the
wood had eaten every one.

"우린 곧 이 숲속을 빠져 나갈수 있을거야," 헨젤이
말했어요.
아이들은 삼일이나 숲속을 헤메었어요. 배 고프고 지쳐,
산딸기를 따먹고, 밤은 나무 밑에서 지새웠어요.
두 아이는 은빛깔 하얀 새들의 노래소리에 잠이 깼어요.
새들을 따라가 보니 한번도 보지 못한 조그만 아름다운
집이 나타났어요.

"We will soon find our way out of this wilderness," said Hansel.
The children searched the woods for three days. Hungry and tired,
feeding only on berries, at last they lay down under a tree to sleep.
They were awakened by the sweet song of a silver white bird. When the
bird flew off into the forest the children followed, until they reached the
most wonderful house they had ever seen.

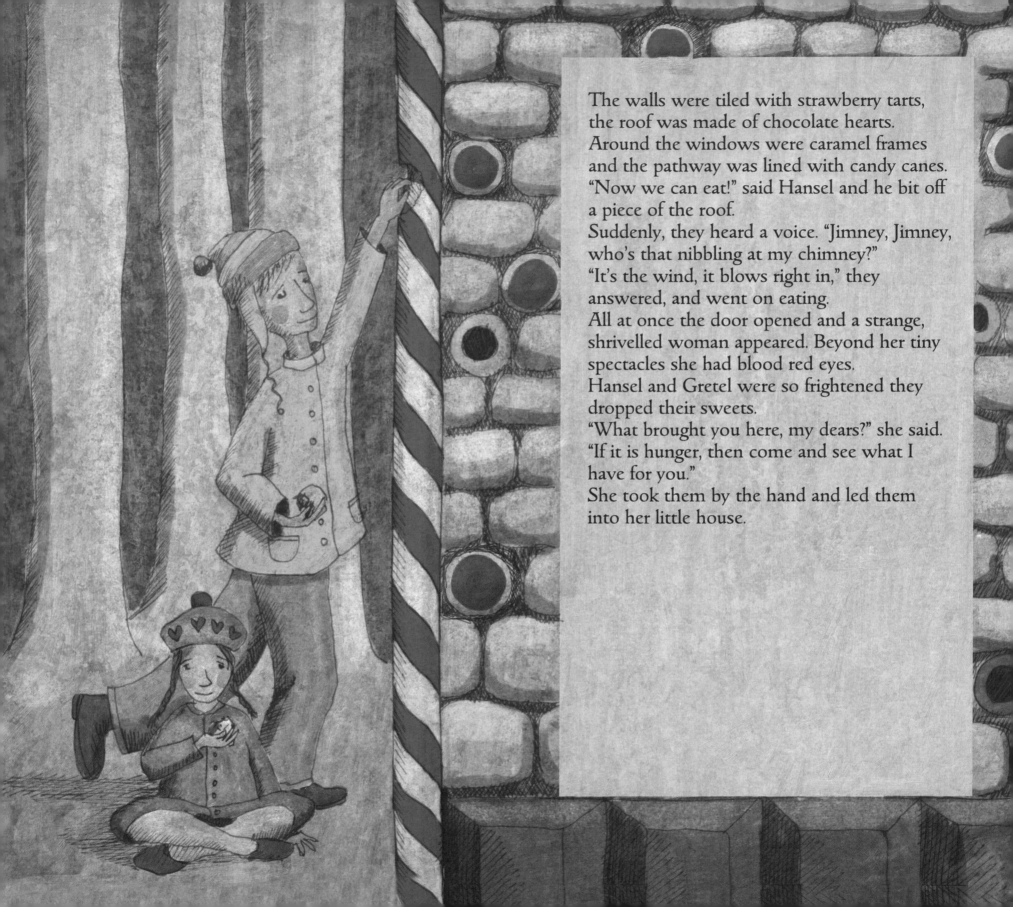

The walls were tiled with strawberry tarts,
the roof was made of chocolate hearts.
Around the windows were caramel frames
and the pathway was lined with candy canes.
"Now we can eat!" said Hansel and he bit off
a piece of the roof.
Suddenly, they heard a voice. "Jimney, Jimney,
who's that nibbling at my chimney?"
"It's the wind, it blows right in," they
answered, and went on eating.
All at once the door opened and a strange,
shrivelled woman appeared. Beyond her tiny
spectacles she had blood red eyes.
Hansel and Gretel were so frightened they
dropped their sweets.
"What brought you here, my dears?" she said.
"If it is hunger, then come and see what I
have for you."
She took them by the hand and led them
into her little house.

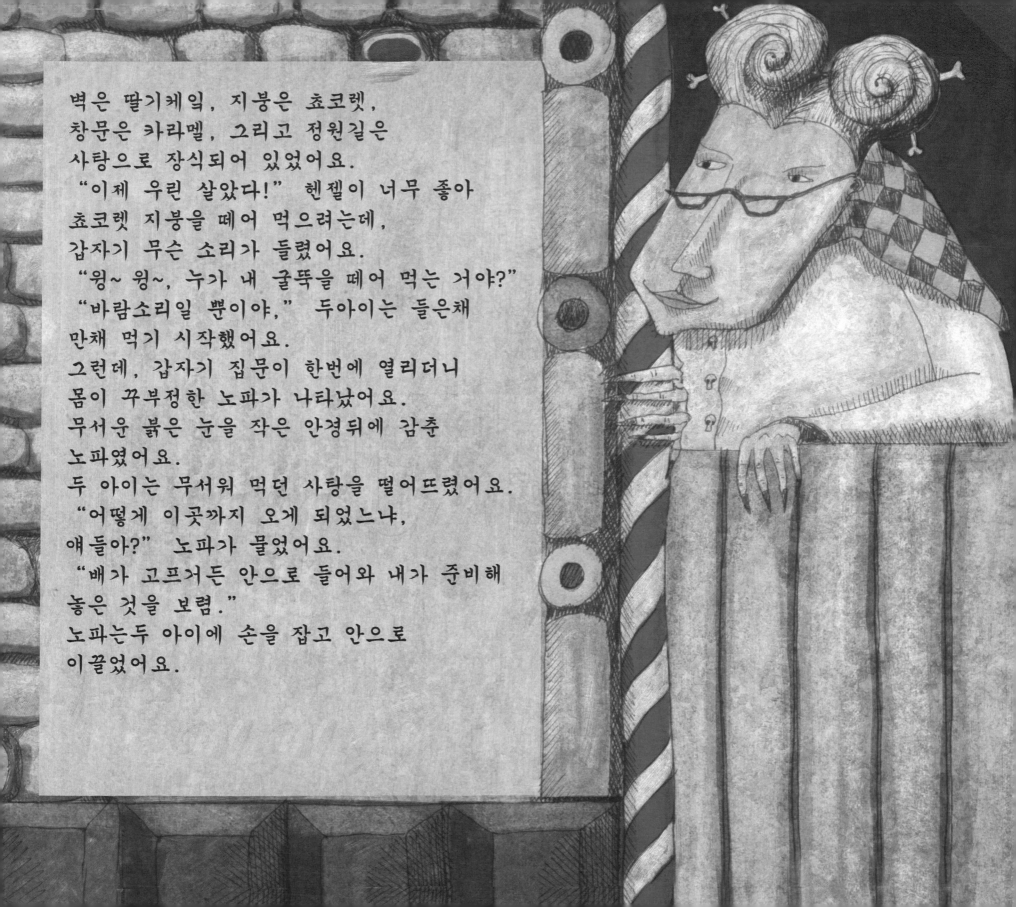

벽은 딸기케잌, 지붕은 쵸코렛,
창문은 카라멜, 그리고 정원길은
사탕으로 장식되어 있었어요.
"이제 우린 살았다!" 헨젤이 너무 좋아
쵸코렛 지붕을 떼어 먹으려는데,
갑자기 무슨 소리가 들렸어요.
"윙~ 윙~, 누가 내 굴뚝을 떼어 먹는 거야?"
"바람소리일 뿐이야," 두아이는 들은채
만채 먹기 시작했어요.
그런데, 갑자기 집문이 한번에 열리더니
몸이 꾸부정한 노파가 나타났어요.
무서운 붉은 눈을 작은 안경뒤에 감춘
노파였어요.
두 아이는 무서워 먹던 사탕을 떨어뜨렸어요.
"어떻게 이곳까지 오게 되었느냐,
얘들아?" 노파가 물었어요.
"배가 고프거든 안으로 들어와 내가 준비해
놓은 것을 보렴."
노파는두 아이에 손을 잡고 안으로
이끌었어요.

두 아이는 노파가 준 맛있는 음식을 먹었어요. 사과, 땅콩, 우유, 그리고 꿀이
발라진 케잌.
배 불리 먹은 아이들은 하얀색 이블로 덮여진 두개의 작은 침대에 누웠어요,
마치 천국 같았어요. 노파는 두 아이 얼굴 가까이 대고 말하길,
"너희 둘 다 너무 말랐어. 오늘은 푹 자거라, 내일부터 공포에 날이 시작될테니!"
먹을것으로 장식된 집, 거짓 친절한 눈이 나쁜 노파. 정말, 무섭다!

Hansel and Gretel were given all good things to eat! Apples and nuts, milk, and pancakes covered
in honey.
Afterwards they lay down in two little beds covered with white linen and slept as though they
were in heaven.
Peering closely at them, the woman said, "You're both so thin. Dream sweet dreams for now,
for tomorrow your nightmares will begin!"
The strange woman with an edible house and poor eyesight had only pretended to be friendly.
Really, she was a wicked witch!

다음날 아침 무서운 노파는 헨젤을 끌고가 새장에 세게 밀어 넣었어요.
새장안에 갇힌 헨젤은 살려달라고 소리쳤어요.
그레텔이 달려왔어요. "왜 우리 오빠를 가둔 거예요?" 그레텔이 울먹였어요.
노파는 붉은 눈을 이리저리 돌리며 비웃으며 말했어요.
"나는 네 오빠를 요리해 먹을거야," 노파가 말했어요. "너는 나를 도울
준비나 해, 요 어린것아."
그레텔은 무서워 어쩔줄 몰랐어요.
노파는 그레텔을 부엌으로 끌고가 오빠에게 먹여 살을 찌울 많은 음식들을
준비하게 했어요.
그러나 헨젤은 음식을 먹지 않았어요.

In the morning the evil witch seized Hansel and shoved him
into a cage. Trapped and terrified he screamed for help.
Gretel came running. "What are you doing to my
brother?" she cried.
The witch laughed and rolled her blood red eyes.
"I'm getting him ready to eat," she replied. "And you're
going to help me, young child."
Gretel was horrified.
She was sent to work in the witch's kitchen where
she prepared great helpings of food for her brother.
But her brother refused to get fat.

노파는 매일 헨젤을 살펴보았어요.
"손가락을 내밀어 봐," 노파는 쏘아대듯, "얼마나
살이 올랐는지 내가 만져 볼수있게!"
헨젤은 주머니 속에 감추어 두었던 닭뼈를 내밀었어요.
눈이 잘 보이지않는 노파는 살이 찌지않는 헨젤을
이해할수 없었어요.
삼일이 지난후 노파는 더이상 기다릴수 없었어요.
"그레텔, 빨리 나무에 불을 붙여, 저 녀석을 요리
냄비에 넣어야 겠다." 노파가 말했어요.

The witch visited Hansel every day. "Stick out your finger,"
she snapped. "So I can feel how plump you are!"
Hansel poked out a lucky wishbone he'd kept in his pocket.
The witch, who as you know had very poor eyesight, just
couldn't understand why the boy stayed boney thin.
After three weeks she lost her patience.
"Gretel, fetch the wood and hurry up, we're going to get
that boy in the cooking pot," said the witch.

그레텔은 일부러 불을 천천히 지피기 시작했어요.
노파는 더이상 참지 못한듯 했어요. "지금이면 오븐 준비가
끝나야 하잖아. 안으로 들어가 요리하기 충분한지 보고와!"
노파는 소리쳤어요.
그레텔은 노파의 조급한 마음을 알았어요. "전 잘 모르겠어요,
충분한지," 그레텔이 말했어요.
"모자란 것, 이 바보같은 것아!" 노파는 소릴 질렀어요.
"오븐문이 이렇게 큰데 그것도 못 보다니, 나 라도 들어갈수
있겠다!"
노파는 보란듯 머리를 오븐 깊숙히 넣었어요.
그레텔은 재빠르게 노파를 훨훨 타오르는 오븐에 밀어 넣었어요.
그레텔은 쇠로된 오븐문을 잠그고 헨젤에게 뛰어가 소리쳤어요.
"노파는 죽었어! 노파는 죽었어! 이제 그 무서운 노파는 없어!"

Gretel slowly stoked the fire for the wood-burning oven.
The witch became impatient. "That oven should be ready by now. Get inside and see if it's hot enough!"
she screamed.
Gretel knew exactly what the witch had in mind. "I don't know how," she said.
"Idiot, you idiot girl!" the witch ranted. "The door is wide enough, even I can get inside!"
And to prove it she stuck her head right in.
Quick as lightning, Gretel pushed the rest of the witch into the burning oven. She shut and bolted the iron
door and ran to Hansel shouting: "The witch is dead! The witch is dead! That's the end of the wicked witch!"

새가 새장을 탈출한듯 헨젤도 새장에서 나와 자유로워 졌어요.

Hansel sprang from the cage like a bird in flight.

두 아이는 서로 안고 좋아했어요. 너무 기뻐 춤도추고
노래도 부르며 껑충껑충 뛰었어요. 두 아이는 집 구석구석
궤속에 가득한 진주, 에머럴드, 루비등 값나가는 보물들을
찾아냈어요. 두 아이는 보석을 주머니 가득 넘치도록
채웠어요.
"우린 많은 보물들을 가졌지만 어떻게 이 깊은 숲속에서
빠져나가지?" 그레텔이 한숨을 내 쉬었어요.
"걱정마, 우린 꼭 집에 돌아갈거야," 헨젤이 말했어요.

Hansel and Gretel hugged each other. They danced and sang and ran
around with joy. In every corner they found treasure chests filled with
pearls, emeralds, rubies and all kinds of worldly precious things. Hansel
and Gretel filled their pockets to overflowing.
"We have wondrous treasures, but how do we escape from the wild
wood?" sighed Gretel.
"Don't worry, together we will find our way home," said Hansel.

두 아이는 세시간을 걸은후 강가에 도착했어요.
"건널수 없을것 같아," 헨젤이 말했어요. "배도 없고, 다리도없어, 흐르는 강물 뿐이야."
"저길봐! 강 건너편을 보라구, 하얀 오리가 물놀이를 하잖아," 그레텔이 말했어요.
"어쩌면오리가 우릴 도와 줄지도 몰라."
두 아이는 입을 모아 노래하듯 오리를 불렀어요: "하얀 날개가 빛나는 오리 아가씨, 제발
저희를 도와 주세요, 강물이 넓고, 깊으니, 저희가 강을 건널수있게 도와주세요?"
오리는 두 아이에게 다가와 먼저 헨젤을 등에 태워 건넜고 그레텔도 안전하게 강을
건너게 해 주었어요. 강 건너편은 와 본듯한 곳이었어요.

After three hours they came upon a stretch of water.
"We cannot cross," said Hansel. "There's no boat, no bridge, just clear blue water."
"Look! Over the ripples, a pure white duck is sailing," said Gretel. "Maybe she can help us."
Together they sang: "Little duck whose white wings glisten, please listen.
The water is deep, the water is wide, could you carry us across to the other side?"
The duck swam towards them and carried first Hansel and then Gretel safely across the water.
On the other side they met a familiar world.

한걸음, 한걸음 두 아이는 마침내 나뭇꾼 아버지의 집을 찾았어요.
"저희 집에 돌아왔어요!" 두 아이는 소리쳤어요.
아버지는 환한 웃음으로 아이들을 맞이했어요. "너희들을 숲에 버린
후 단하루도 행복한 날이 없었단다." 나뭇꾼이 말했어요.
"너희를 찾기위해 않 가본곳이 없을 정도로…"

Step by step, they found their way back to the woodcutter's cottage.
"We're home!" the children shouted.
Their father beamed from ear to ear. "I haven't spent one happy moment since you've been gone," he said.
"I searched, everywhere…"

"새 어머니는요?"
"그 여자는 떠났어! 먹을것이떨어지자 화를 내며 가 버렸어, 그 여자를 다시는 만나지 않을거란다. 이제 우리 셋이 행복하게 살자꾸나."
"이젠 우리 보물도 많아요," 헨젤이 주머니속의 눈처럼 하얀진주를 꺼내 보이며 말했어요.
"와," 아버지가 놀라 말하기를, "이제 우리의 가난은 끝이 난것 같구나!"

"And Mother?"
"She's gone! When there was nothing left to eat she stormed out saying I would never see her again. Now there are just the three of us."
"And our precious gems," said Hansel as he slipped a hand into his pocket and produced a snow white pearl.
"Well," said their father, "it seems all our problems are at an end!"